First Published in 2017 by SQ Magazine

This edition published in 2026 by Stone Orchid Press LLC

Print ISBN: 979-8-9955708-0-6

Ebook ISBN: 978-1-7344367-9-2

Audiobook ISBN: 979-8-9955708-1-3

Cover design by GetCovers.com

Published by Stone Orchid Press LLC

https://jodilmilner.com/

The Skull Collector

The young man's corpse washed ashore in the hushed chill of morning. The Shaman had been waiting, watching for the body through the long hours of the night. The sight brought the dread of the lies he would be forced to tell the tribe. He carried the youth, who through his aging eye appeared no more than a boy, from the waves and placed him on top of the prepared funeral pyre.

His striking flint and steel felt too worn in his hands. He had lit too many of these fires on this sacred beach with only inquisitive sand crabs for company. This winter ritual, this lie about earning the right to journey to the Golden Island, was wrong. If the gods wished the tribe to sacrifice the youth, they deserved to know their fate. Ages ago, before the Shaman's birth, many died trying to reach the island every year. His father, who served as shaman before him, convinced the tribe that holding a contest would better please the gods. At least then, only one would die.

A brilliant spark caught on the coconut fiber kindling and red tendrils of fire snaked through the bundle in his hands. He coaxed the fire brighter with a soft puff of air before adding it to the larger slivers of wood. Soon, the pile blazed hot and bright, sending a tower of smoke high into the sky that would be seen for miles. The villagers, gathered on the other side of the steep rocky ridge dividing them from this sacred space, would see the smoke and know that all was well.

The flames licked around the limbs of the dead, a young man named Siaki. He deserved to be chosen. He had proven himself and brought much honor to his family as he perfected his skills and mastered his use of tools and weapons alike. In many ways, he reminded the Shaman of his own son.

The smell of charred flesh stuck to the Shaman's hair and clothes and crept down his throat. In the bitterness of the morning, he questioned his loyalty to the village and to the gods. What would happen if they learned that Siaki never reached his promised paradise?

The fire died down, leaving greasy blackened bones and gristle on the ashes. He carried them one armful at a time to a hidden area of the palm forest where the ants hunted.

They could be trusted with cleaning the bones before they were ground to powder and mixed into the sand of the beach.

He placed the last bone, Siaki's skull, at the base of the tallest palm and cradled it into a depression in the sand. There, he knelt and offered one last prayer for the safe passage of Siaki's soul to the afterlife.

The stink of death clung to the Shaman's skin, forcing him to wash himself before taking up his totems and ceremonial dress once more. He lifted the beaded and feathered chest piece and set it on his shoulders, feeling the weight settle against his bare skin, a weight meant to represent the solemnity of his office. The feathered head piece pinched at his temples, a constant reminder of his duty to be an example of humility and devotion. He hated the last piece the most. The staff of crooked driftwood, which bore rows upon rows of elaborate weavings and beadwork. Each duty he fulfilled, each birth, each successful harvest, and each winter ritual added another narrow band of color.

He lifted the staff to his shoulder. The walk back to the village from the secluded beach pressed harder against his heart with each passing year.

Siaki's family would be waiting for him. He would have to reassure them that their beloved child had indeed reached the distant shore of the Golden Island. The lie came harder every year.

Only one person took the sting of his duty away, at least for a time. Makana with the silken shoulders, his wife, waited under the lip of the rise, as she had each year since the day they had been joined as man and wife.

She stood and laced her hand in his, showing no sign of impatience at having waited several hours.

"Is he well?" she asked.

Lying to her hurt most of all. To speak the truth would rob the sparkle from her eyes. *How could she love one who allowed such a horror to continue?*

"He is in his new home now. May his soul find happiness there." The lie brought with it a taste of ash and bile in his throat.

She pointed along the beach. "Your son is eager to see you."

Liko held a collection of two-pronged spears and stood on the edge of a rock as he studied the water. With one smooth motion, he flung the spear and pulled out a brilliant silver wriggling fish.

The Shaman rubbed at the tense spot between his eyes. For the last several years, Liko had been asking to come with him and learn how to give the ceremonial offerings on behalf of the one traveling to the island.

"How long did he stay awake waiting for me?" he asked.

"Until nearly morning. He would have made it longer, had he not spent most of the night celebrating around the fires."

"Is he disappointed?"

"Why could he not come this year?" Makana's tone sharpened and her arms crossed over her bosom. "You have trained him in everything else, is there a reason he must wait for this?"

The Shaman leaned against one of the dark volcanic rocks, drawing strength from its solid mass. After the long terrible night it would be too easy to become cross. "There is a time for everything. I will not change my mind about this. He cannot come with me until after he competes for his chance to go to the Golden Island next year." Even as the words left his mouth he felt the weight press on his chest. *How could the gods expect him to allow his son to die for nothing?* He cleared his throat. "Next year, should he not be the victor, I will take him to pray with me."

She shook her head, unpleased with his answer and turned her attention to the hut behind them. "There is food inside, when you are ready. You best get something to eat and rest a while before he learns that you have returned. I am sure he will have questions upon questions for you."

"It can wait until after I have spoken with Siaki's family. They have been patient."

Maintaining a serene face, despite the raging storm of emotion that threatened to overwhelm him, took energy that the Shaman did not have. Facing the family of a boy that he knew was dead would test him once more. He could not let them lose the hope that their son lived on in paradise. Having a child chosen from among all the youth brought the family great honor.

The sight of the family, so content, so at peace, made the Shaman wish the gods would allow at least one of these youth to reach the shore instead of claiming them all. It was by the grace of the gods that they knew of the Golden Island. It was by their hands that the sun shone through the narrow pass between the twin sleeping volcanos and made the promised island appear and shine like fire.

He bowed his head to the father of the family. "Congratulations, your son has joined a legacy of our people to attain the Golden Island. You should be very proud."

The father brought his hand over his heart and bowed in return. "You honor us."

The Shaman raised his hand in acknowledgment. "It is a deserved honor. Will your family be well without Siaki's help?"

"Well enough. It will take getting used to not having him bringing his share of fresh fish and coconuts, but my younger son is strong and smart. With time, he will do very well."

"And your daughter? Next year it will be her turn to compete, how do you think she will fare?"

"Kaha'i wishes to please the gods but has never felt the pull of the island, not like the boys. She will do us proud, but many can best her. It is for the best, her mother would miss her terribly." Siaki's father glanced back to where his wife and daughter worked at slicing green bananas and folding them in long fronds for the fire. "Liko will be in the contest next year. Is he keen on attaining the island?"

The Shaman fought to keep his face smooth and untroubled. "Too much I think. He is determined to prove himself."

"Like his dad then?"

"Better, he has talent." The Shaman forced a laugh. "Must get it from his mother."

"Your family will be honored should he win."

"We shall see. No one knows what the future holds." The Shaman gave a short bow and turned before Siaki's father could continue talking of the future.

When the Shaman returned to his hut he found Liko pacing back and forth, deep in thought. He cleared his throat, making the boy jump.

Liko touched his forehead and gave a respectful bow. "I am glad you have returned."

The Shaman selected one of the leaf-wrapped morsels from the basket in the center of the small space. "I am sure you have." He opened the leaf to find a piece of beautifully cooked fish.

As expected, Liko wasted no time before starting in with his questions. "Learning the prayers for those traveling to the Golden Island is the only rite remaining before I can take my place beside you as younger shaman. Why could I not come this year?" He stared straight into the Shaman's eyes, unflinching and firm, qualities. "I need a good reason."

The Shaman arched an eyebrow. Ever since the boy had earned his first feathers, he had tested his limits. At least he never tried to fight. Showing disrespect would lower his standing in the tribe's eyes.

"Since when do you get to decide when to learn the parts of your trade?" He proceeded carefully, each word measured and delivered with quiet precision.

The boy quieted his anger immediately as he remembered his place. "I am sorry, I only meant that I have learned so much. I have memorized every rite and every gesture. I have done everything you have ever asked. I thought that this year, especially since there is the chance I will be leaving, that you would teach me this last ritual." He cast his gaze out the open door and toward the sea. "It would surely please the gods for me to complete my training, would it not?"

The ache to tell his son the truth squeezed at the Shaman's heart. If the boy knew, all his uncertainty would disappear. He would stop this crazy quest to be the best and learn to enjoy life one day at a time.

"I have already told your mother, should you not be chosen next year I will show you what must be done. Until then, I urge you to practice patience and humility. They are both vital in the life of a Shaman."

The son gave another bow, so formal, too formal. The Shaman wished he could hold Liko in his arms like he used to when the boy was small. There would be so few chances left to spend time with him. The next winter equinox would come far too fast and with it, the return of the island.

Weeks had passed when the Shaman finally returned to retrieve Siaki's skull, now grey and picked clean. He could not help but think that the next skull he recovered would be that of his own son. He pushed the thought from his mind. Grieving something that was not certain would only poison the remaining months before the contest. With a sharp stylus, he inscribed the bone with Siaki's life, his name, and his deeds.

When the tide dropped low, he walked out into the water and ducked under the waves to the hidden entrance of the cave. He pushed through the darkness, feeling the familiar pain of air burning in his lungs. Inside the cave, a dim light filtered down from a small opening high above. Dozens of skulls lined the walls, too many. The Shaman could not bring himself to count them, as if knowing the exact number would make him personally accountable for each death.

Knowing that his father before him had done the same grim task alone, for so many years, eased the burden.

With a sigh, he set Siaki's skull high on a ledge where the light would touch it from time to time. He allowed himself to imagine the future when Liko would be entrusted with the same secret about the contest and would learn how to prepare the dead as a sacrifice to the gods. Then, he would no longer have to bear the terrible burden alone.

Days and weeks passed, fast and steady like the tide. For the children reaching their seventeenth cycle, this was the last chance to prove themselves worthy of taking part in the yearly contest. Liko stood tall, a rare pearl among the oysters, his great shoulders a testament to the many hours spent swimming across the bay and diving deep for abalone.

The nights grew cooler and the sun's rays at sunset crept closer and closer toward the notch between the two mounts. Each evening, when the sun dipped low to the horizon, the Shaman measured the path of light and shadow. As much as he wished it, he could not stop the sun from moving, just as he could not stop the wind or waves.

The Shaman approached the tribal elders at the evening meal. "It is time to select those who will honor the gods on our behalf, the Golden Island will appear in two days."

The announcement brought a chorus of cheers from the assembled families. Runners leapt up from around the fire, like flying embers, to notify those living on other parts of the isle. Makana and Liko cheered along with the rest while the Shaman held his silence. At times like these, the Shaman was grateful for the solemn nature of his position. Nothing could have felt more wrong than cheering for the death of yet another child.

Makana leaned in close. She had daggers hidden in her smile. "Smile for your son. He has waited his whole life for this."

He pressed his lips into what he hoped would pass as a smile. "Forgive me. Old habit I guess." Before he could say more, the wail of a conch shell sounded nearby. "The elders are meeting, I must go."

Makana clung to his hand as he turned to leave. "Liko wants this. Please, speak well of him."

"Of course," he said, giving her hand one last squeeze. She did not know that as Liko's father he was not allowed to speak on his son's behalf, a fact he was very grateful for. Not being forced to choose and debate over his son's life relieved a small portion of the anguish that had already wormed its way deep within his gut.

The council debated long into the night, as they had done each year. Only the best of the youth could be chosen. Allowing those who had not shown enough devotion, offended the gods. Those early hours weighed heavy on the Shaman. Liko numbered among those chosen, as he had known he would. The boy had earned it. It was his right and privilege to honor the family.

When the council adjourned, the Shaman could not rest. He wandered the island until he found himself on the sacred ground of the isolated beach. There, he fell to his knees and offered his strongest prayers to the gods that his son not be taken from him. Not yet. There was still honor in being chosen and not winning the right to swim to the Golden Island.

When the morning came, the Shaman returned home. He could not bear to watch while Makana readied Liko. She rubbed his skin with fragrant oils and braided his hair into neat rows adorned with beads and feathers. He excused himself from their hut, pleading that he needed to offer another prayer for Liko's sake.

Morning progressed and more and more people gathered on the beach. Small knots formed around the youth in their elaborate costumes. A cluster of children stood in awe around Liko along with a sizable group of girls who had already passed their seventeenth year.

Another conch sounded and the twenty-seven youth stepped forward and stood in a line waiting for the elders to make their choice. Their skin shone brilliant in the morning sun and the beads in their hair rustled in the ocean breeze.

One by one, the elders walked the line, pulling those chosen forward. As they approached Liko, the Shaman met the boy's gaze. He had expected to see fear there, as he had seen in so many of the other boys and girls. Instead, Liko's gaze was firm and steady, showing nothing of what he must be feeling inside as the elders pulled him forward.

In the crowd, tears of pride ran down Makana's face. If the Shaman did not give some sign of his approval, she would never forgive him. He met Liko's gaze once more and gave him a nod. Thoughts of having to burn his son's body made it hard to do anything more. Still, when Liko saw it, he smiled wide enough to show all of his gleaming white teeth.

With the selection finished, the council wasted no time in organizing the first event: a race around the perimeter of the island. The twelve selected youth toed the line drawn in the sand, their eyes locked on the elder who stood out front with a stout walking stick stretched high before him. The crowd went silent, waiting for his signal.

The stick fell. When it touched the sand, the twelve ran, churning up clouds with their bare feet. Younger brothers and sisters ran to the steep sides of the closer sister volcano to watch as their siblings made the circuit, calling out who was in the lead to those waiting below.

The Shaman did not strain his ears like the others to hear, like his wife did, but he could tell from the happy glances, from the encouraging shouts, that Liko was in the lead.

Makana glared at him when she noticed. "Why can you not be happy that he is doing well?" she said between her teeth so those standing near could not hear.

The Shaman forced a smile although he knew his eyes betrayed him. "I am pleased that he is doing well. I could not be prouder as a father."

"Liar." Her voice betrayed a hurt that she had done so well to hide before. "He has never been enough for you has he? Even now when he is proving himself in front of the whole tribe, he is not enough, is he? Not for you." She sniffed and her shoulders drooped. "You know he only does it for your approval. Your opinion of him is all that matters. He will kill himself trying to get a kind word from you."

Her revelation yanked an involuntary gasp from his lips. All these years he had withheld his approval in hopes that Liko would rebel and spend his energy in anger instead of excelling at whatever task he was given. Learning that it had the opposite effect, that his disapproval was what pushed Liko harder than the other children, made the Shaman's hands shake.

A shout arose from the far edge of the beach as competitors rounded the final corner. Liko led the pack with another boy following close on his heels. The last stretch returned the runners to the soft sands of the beach. The Shaman silently willed Liko to trip, so that anyone other than him would win.

Fate has a funny way of working against one's desires. The stronger the Shaman pleaded for his son to fall, the faster his son moved until he seemed to soar like a long-winged albatross. The other boy had no chance against Liko's swift strides.

Other events such as swimming, fishing, and wrestling came and went filling that day and most of the next. The Shaman struggled to bring himself to watch, knowing that each victory brought the boy that much closer to his death.

At the end of the afternoon, Liko stood with his head held high. He had won.

People, hundreds of them, swept around Liko, eager to congratulate him on a job well done. They pushed past the Shaman who could not bring himself to move. It was no surprise Liko won. However, he had prayed so many times for it not to happen that he could not help but feel betrayed.

A frail hand tugged on his elbow. Elder Iana, the eldest of the council, was so old and bent that his white tufted head only reached the Shaman's shoulder. He beckoned him to come away from the crowd.

"Your father would be proud of him, as should you. Why do you look so glum?"

"I can not let him die."

Iana whacked him on the shoulder. "You swore to never speak of it."

"And I have kept my oath. You are the only one left who knows the truth."

"And I also know this is still the best way to keep the gods happy." Liko gripped his shoulder tighter. "You would not understand how I do. In your father's time, dozens would enter the water every year and all would die. The solution is not perfect. The gods are very picky who they choose. We can not let the tribe lose their faith."

"The gods have not chosen a single one in all my years as Shaman. What am I supposed to believe?"

Iana patted his heart. "The tribe is peaceful and thriving. They believe that they are doing what is right. The youth are stronger and smarter than ever. None of this would have happened if we did not start the contest. Your son would have sacrificed himself years ago had things continued as they had. Be grateful for this extra time you have been granted."

A shout came from further up the beach. The Shaman did not need to look to know that the Golden Island had appeared in the distance. The tribe would be waiting for him to perform the farewell ceremony.

Iana waved him away. "Go. Liko needs you. Your wife needs you. Your people need you."

The Shaman wrapped his hand around his staff, feeling each of the bands under his palm, each death, each birth, and each sickness. How could he be a spiritual leader if he did not believe?

The crowd parted to either side, letting him pass through to the clearing where Liko and Makana stood.

He held his arms out wide and the noise of the crowd quieted. The ceremonial words came unbidden to his tongue and flowed from his lips. So many years he had stood in the same place, saying the same words, all the while knowing it would be the last time he would see that year's champion alive.

How dare his tongue make saying those same words to his son effortless!

"Liko, we have come together to celebrate your devotion to the gods. By the knowledge you possess in your mind and the strength of your body you have shown your worth to your tribe. I will now grant you one final blessing." He touched Liko's brow. "May your mind remember the family you are leaving behind." He moved his hand to the crest of Liko's shoulder. "May your arms stay strong to build goodness into this world." Next, the legs. "May your legs carry you to where you are needed." And finally, the heart. The Shaman took a steadying breath as he felt its steady rhythm beneath his palm. "May your heart stay true to the path that the gods have laid out for you."

Liko bowed low, his hand pressed against his chest in respect. "I will make you proud, father."

The Shaman took Liko and wrapped him in his arms. It was not part of the blessing, but he could not let his boy go without one last embrace, without letting him know how he felt. "You have always made me proud."

When they released each other the crowd surged again, forcing them apart and urging Liko into the waves. After one last goodbye wave, he dove into the water and was gone.

Someone tugged on the Shaman's hand, pulling him away from the crowd. When he turned, he saw fear in his wife's eyes for the first time. "Come, you must pray for him that he might be guided tonight."

Had it been possible, he would have stayed by her side for the long night as she waited and worried. His promise was the best comfort he could give her. "Wait for me on the rise. I will return as soon as he is safe."

That night, it was not his place to break her heart. He slipped away and over the ridge where the village believed he did everything in his power to protect and guide the victor in their journey. He could hold on to his secret as long as he needed to, there was far more happiness in thinking that their son had left to a better place.

Back on the isolated beach, accompanied by the whispers of the sea, the Shaman constructed the funeral pyre one heavy log at a time. The last thing he could offer his son was a steady strong fire to consume his body and send his soul rising and spiraling up into the heavens.

When the pyre was finished, he made a nest from the fibers of a coconut husk for kindling and knelt in the sand of the beach. Even with his faith broken, he would continue to pray on behalf of his son as he waited and watched for the boy's body to return. It would be hours yet. The night darkened and the stars made their slow march overhead. Each year, for the past thirty years, the body had always returned in the hour before the rising of the sun.

However, when the morning light spilled over the edge of the sea there was still no sign of Liko. The thought of the gods accepting his son when they had rejected so many should have brought him happiness. Instead, it filled him with horror. The boy should have died and his body returned safely to shore. The Shaman's prayers had gone unanswered for so long that he was convinced the gods had stopped listening ages ago. He continued to try. The people needed his devotion to fortify their own.

The Shaman walked the length of the beach, searching the rocks and around the base of the cliffs for any sign of his son. He would never forgive himself if Liko's body was out there and he overlooked it.

He paced the length of the beach once more, allowing another, and another, hour to pass. The village expected to see the smoke from his fire to signal that all was well, but with no body to burn, the Shaman questioned whether he should wait longer or go ahead and light the blaze.

His thoughts drifted to Makana waiting for the sign, waiting for him, on the other side of the ridge. Whatever fears haunted him, he knew hers would be worse. Every moment he delayed caused her greater pain. She needed to believe all was well, that Liko had reached a better place. Perhaps he had.

The Shaman set his flint into the nest of kindling at the base of the pyre. Soon, thick smoke rose into the sky. Only then, did the Shaman allow himself to mourn the loss of his son. With all of the other children, he knew the certainty of their fate. He took great care that their bodies received the respect they deserved. Not being able to do the same for his son left him hollow inside.

The heat from the fire dried the tears that would not stop flowing. For so long, he had prepared his heart for the day when he would be the one to burn his son's body and commit his bones to the sand of the beach. He could never have prepared himself for this.

The fire burned to ash. The emptiness remained. He wanted to curse the gods for burdening him with these new doubts. Had they been waiting all this time for the proper sacrifice? Why his child? Why not any of the others?

Elder Iana and his own father had always taught that this life was a test. Had the gods been testing him all this time? If it had been a test, what was he supposed to learn? His son was gone and he was not sure where.

The totems of the Shaman's office rested in the sand at the base of the ridge that separated him from the village. He took up the heavy chest piece, the headdress that pinched, and finally the staff. Another band of color would be added to join the dozens of others.

Liko's band.

Free Story

Choose an exclusive short story when you join my reader newsletter.

jodilmilner.com/free-story

Also by Jodi L. Milner

<u>The Shadow Barrier Trilogy</u>

Stonebearer's Betrayal

Stonebearer's Apprentice

Stonebearer's Redemption

<u>Complete Omnibus Edition</u>

The Complete Shadow Barrier Trilogy: An Epic Coming of

Age Fantasy Saga

(Includes bonus prequel and epilogue stories)

<u>Other Published Fiction</u>

Breath: A Creation Myth Short Story

The Skull Collector

Reviews

If you enjoyed The Skull Collector, please consider leaving a review at your favorite retailer. Even a few words can help other readers discover the story.

Thank you for supporting independent authors.

Author's Note

The Skull Collector was originally published in *SQ Magazine* in June of 2017, months before the ezine stopped publishing. I've always loved the story and was thrilled for it to be included on a platform where fellow lovers of speculative fiction could find it.

The story itself came to me during one of the rare times I've attempted a writing exercise. The exercise is simple: write down a word for each letter of the alphabet, in order, as fast as you can. Then do it again. And again a third time. The first list cleans out the cobwebs (mine, strangely enough, is usually full of the names of different foods). During the second list, the mind begins to loosen up. By the third, ideas start rising to the surface.

Of all the words that surfaced during that exercise, the ones that lingered were volcano, island, and equinox. With those ideas priming the pump, the story came together fairly quickly and carried with it that mix of bittersweet tension and family drama that I'm always drawn to explore.

Looking back on the story now, what surprises me most is not how quickly it came together, but how stubbornly it has stayed with me. At its heart, The Skull Collector is about inheritance: what we're given, what we keep, and what we might be better off setting down. It asks, in its own way, how much of the past we owe our loyalty to, and how much we're allowed to leave behind.

Jodi

About the Author

Jodi L Milner, author of the award-winning Shadow Barrier Trilogy, wanted to be a superhero and a doctor when she grew up. Upon discovering she couldn't fly, she did what any reasonable introvert would do and escaped into the wonderful hero-filled world of fiction and the occasional medical journal. She's lived there ever since.

These days, when she's not folding the children or feeding the laundry, she creates her own noble heroes on the page. Her short stories explore the fabric of dreams, while her novels weave magic into what it means to be human.

Jodi is a firm believer that life is what you make it, and she intends to make it a good one. She is an avid student of the interesting and obscure and has an unhealthy fascination with mental health and medical science. This path led to her working professionally in both human and animal medicine.

She still dreams of flying.

Learn more at JodiLMilner.com